Our Tree Named
STEVE

Alan Zweibel

Illustrated by

David Catrow

PUFFIN BOOKS

Dear Kids,

A long time ago, when you were little, Mom and I took you to where we wanted to build a house for us to live in.

But in order to build there, men had to come and clear the land.

I remember there was one tree, however, that the three of you couldn't stop staring at. Adam thought it was crying, Lindsay said it looked nervous, and Sari, who was only two years old, couldn't pronounce the word *tree*, and called it "Steve."

"I love you, Steve," she kept saying. And then Adam and Lindsay
started saying it. And before too long, Mom and I got the hint and
asked the builder to please save Steve.

The day we moved in, Steve was there to greet us.

He quickly worked his way into your lives as a swing holder,

target, third base, hiding place, jump-rope turner . . .

. . . and whenever our dryer broke down,

he held our underwear with pride.

Yes, right there in the center of our yard, this weird-looking tree grew to become the center of our outdoor life.

Through all our barbecues, campouts, dance parties . . .

. . . or when Adam and Lindsay started getting crushes on the
Simon kids next door, Steve adjusted to our every need.

And it wasn't always easy. Standing tall through snowstorms
in the winter . . .

. . . or when Uncle Chester napped in the hammock couldn't possibly have been fun.

Not to mention the time that the sewer overflowed and Steve sucked up all the smelly water before it drowned Kirby . . .

. . . then got so sick himself that the tree doctor had to give Steve a haircut that made him look like a big thumb.

Through the years Mom and I have tried to show you, in a world filled with strangers, the peace that comes with having things you can count on and a safe place to return to after a hard day or a long trip.

Which brings me to the point of this letter. Last week, a storm hit our area . . .

. . . and though we spared Steve's life a long time ago,

this time we couldn't save him.

Are we sad? Sure we are. But even in his final moments, when
he could have fallen on our house, Sari's swings, Kirby's house,

or Mom's garden, Steve performed his last trick and protected
all of us to the very end, and friends like this are hard to find.

So, when you come home from Grandma's next week, Steve will not be able to greet you as he's done in the past. I'm sorry.

But please know that Steve will always be with us.
In our hearts, in our thoughts . . .

. . . and in a different tree at the
other end of our yard.
See you next week.
Love,
Dad

To Robin, Adam, Lindsay, Sari, and Kirby

—A. Z.

To Deborah, for standing by me through all our storms

—D. C.

PUFFIN BOOKS
Published by the Penguin Group
Penguin Young Readers Group, 345 Hudson Street, New York, New York 10014, U.S.A.
Penguin Group (Canada), 90 Eglinton Avenue East, Suite 700, Toronto, Ontario, Canada M4P 2Y3 (a division of Pearson Penguin Canada Inc.)
Penguin Books Ltd, 80 Strand, London WC2R 0RL, England
Penguin Ireland, 25 St Stephen's Green, Dublin 2, Ireland (a division of Penguin Books Ltd)
Penguin Group (Australia), 250 Camberwell Road, Camberwell, Victoria 3124, Australia (a division of Pearson Australia Group Pty Ltd)
Penguin Books India Pvt Ltd, 11 Community Centre, Panchsheel Park, New Delhi - 110 017, India
Penguin Group (NZ), Cnr Airborne and Rosedale Roads, Albany, Auckland 1310, New Zealand (a division of Pearson New Zealand Ltd)
Penguin Books (South Africa) (Pty) Ltd, 24 Sturdee Avenue, Rosebank, Johannesburg 2196, South Africa

Registered Offices: Penguin Books Ltd, 80 Strand, London WC2R 0RL, England

First published in the United States of America by G. P. Putnam's Sons, a division of Penguin Young Readers Group, 2005
Published by Puffin Books, a division of Penguin Young Readers Group, 2007

30 29 28
RRD

Text copyright © Alan Zweibel, 2005
Illustrations copyright © David Catrow, 2005
All rights reserved

THE LIBRARY OF CONGRESS HAS CATALOGED THE G. P. PUTNAM'S SONS EDITION AS FOLLOWS:
Zweibel, Alan.
Our tree named Steve / Alan Zweibel ; illustrated by David Catrow.
p. cm.
Summary: In a letter to his children, a father recounts memories of the role Steve, the tree in their front yard, has played in their lives.
[1. Trees—Fiction. 2. Family life—Fiction. 3. Letters—Fiction.]
I. Catrow, David, ill. II. Title.
PZ7.Z8480u 2005 [E]—dc22 2004001891
ISBN: 0-399-23722-4 (hc)
Designed by Gina DiMassi.
Text set in Andy Bold.
The art was done in pencil and watercolor.

Puffin Books ISBN 978-0-14-240743-1
Manufactured in China